This Walker book belongs to:

_____

_____

_____

First published 2009 by Walker Books Ltd

87 Vauxhall Walk, London SE11 5HJ

This edition published 2010

2 4 6 8 10 9 7 5 3 1

Text © 2009 Colin McNaughton

Illustrations © 2009 Emma Chichester Clark

British Library Cataloguing in Publication Data:

a catalogue record for this book is available from the British Library

ISBN 978-1-4063-2556-0

www.walker.co.uk

WALKER BOOKS
AND SUBSIDIARIES

LONDON • BOSTON • SYDNEY • AUCKLAND

NOT LAST NIGHT
BUT THE NIGHT BEFORE

Colin McNaughton

Illustrated by Emma Chichester Clark

For Coline and Gabin
C.M.

For William and Peter
E.C.C.

Not last night but the night before,
Three black cats came knocking at the door.

I came downstairs to let them in,
They knocked me down like a bowling pin.

Not last night but the night before,
The man in the moon came knocking at the door.

He rushed right in, he didn't stop,

He spun me round like a spinning top.

Not last night but the night before,
Three little pigs came knocking at the door.

They roared right in like a choo-choo train
And knocked me down on my back again.

Not last night but the night before,
Little Bo-peep came knocking at the door.

Goodness gracious, fancy that,
She bundled in and knocked me flat.

(She'd found her sheep.)

Not last night but the night before,
Little Miss Muffet came knocking at the door.

I opened the door – she opened it wider –
And I got squished by a big fat spider.

Not last night but the night before,
Jack and Jill came knocking at the door.

Jack rolled in, shrieked with laughter,
Sister Jill came tumbling after.

Not last night but the night before,
Three blind mice came knocking at the door.

The farmer's wife, oh fiddle-dee-dee!

I saw her but she didn't see me.

(See how they run!)

Not last night but the night before,
Goldilocks came knocking at the door.

I thought that she'd come on her own,
Crash! Bang! Wallop! Well I might have known.

Not last night but the night before,
Mister Punch came knocking at the door.

Judy, Baby, Crocodile too,

Said, "Good evening – how do you do?"

(Now that's the way to do it!)

Not last night but the night before,

There was no more knocking on my front door.

A glass was tapped – ting-ting-ting!

And all of a sudden they began to sing...

Happy birthday to you

Squashed tomatoes and stew

Bread and butter in the gutter

Happy birthday to you!

Not last night but the night before,

I spread my gifts on the bedroom floor.

The house was still – there wasn't a peep.

I went to bed and I fell ... asleep!

Other books by Colin McNaughton

978-1-4063-1352-9

978-0-7445-4394-0

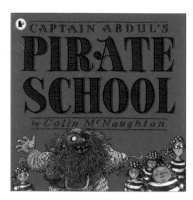

978-0-7445-9896-4

978-1-4063-0585-2

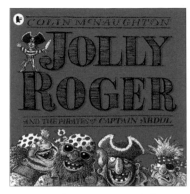

978-1-84428-478-8

Also by Emma Chichester Clark

978-1-4063-0417-6

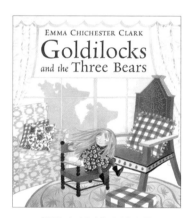

978-1-4063-1484-7

Available from all good bookstores

www.walker.co.uk